Angel
Hide and Seek

by Ann Turner

illustrated by Lois Ehlert

HarperCollins*Publishers*

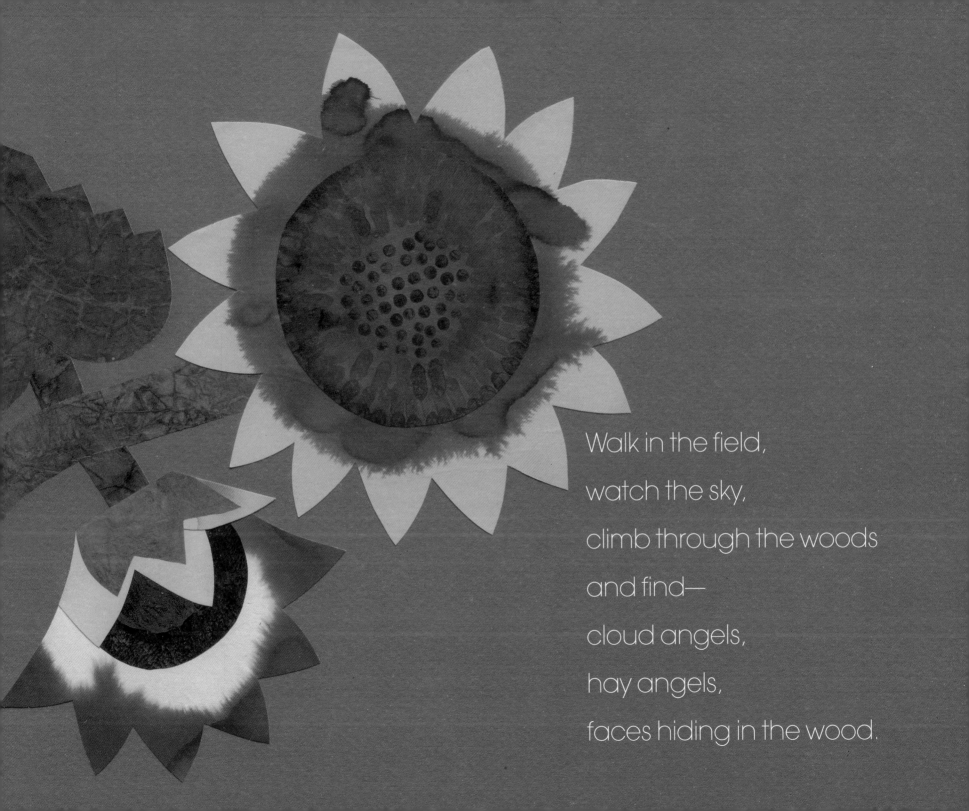

Walk in the field,

watch the sky,

climb through the woods

and find—

cloud angels,

hay angels,

faces hiding in the wood.

Sunflower
Angels

Petal halos glow
around their heads,
as their faces nod
and bend.

Barn
Angels

On the side of the barn
the wood is silver
and striped with light.
Watch the shadows move—
is something hiding there?

Hay Angel

In the back field

the tractor leaves

piles of green hay.

In one, my sister sweeps

her arms up and down.

"Look, a hay angel!"

And the black-eyed Susans

are a bright halo.

Butterfly
Angel

On a day

when the sky is

blue as paint,

orange and black wings

surprise my eyes.

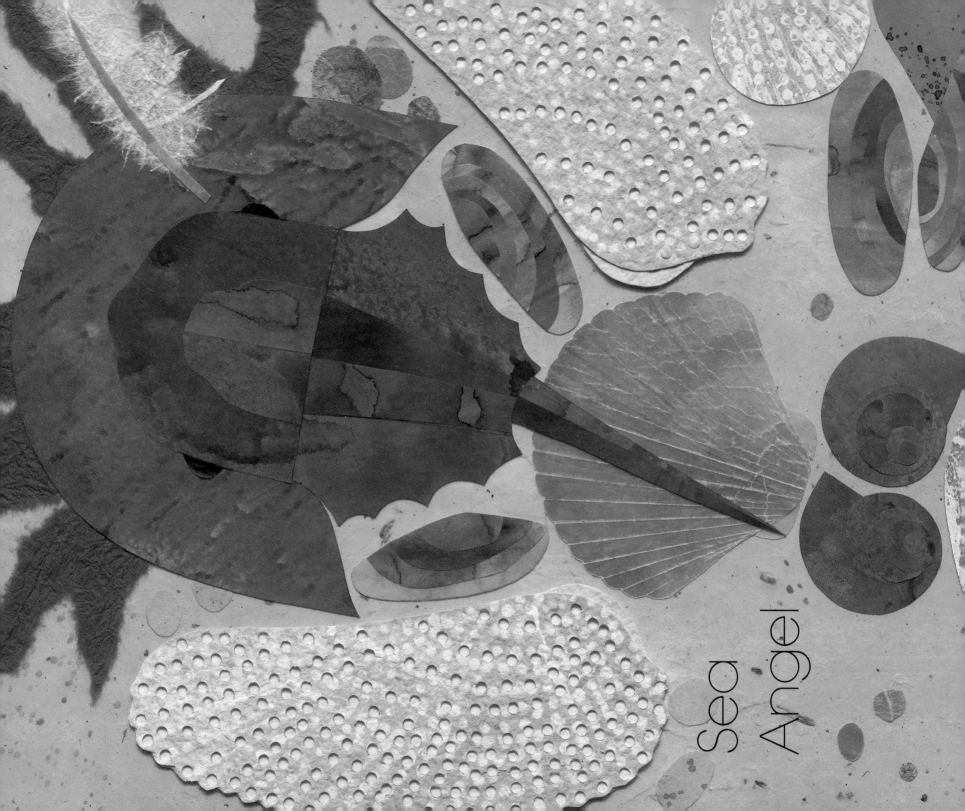

Sea
Angel

We went treasure hunting

by the shore

and made a picture

on the sand:

a horseshoe crab

for the head,

a scatter of shells for wings,

and a hank of green weed

for the sea angel's hair.

Wood Angels

I find a pile

of leaves and nuts

and pinecone petals

scattered together—

small faces

hiding in the wild wood.

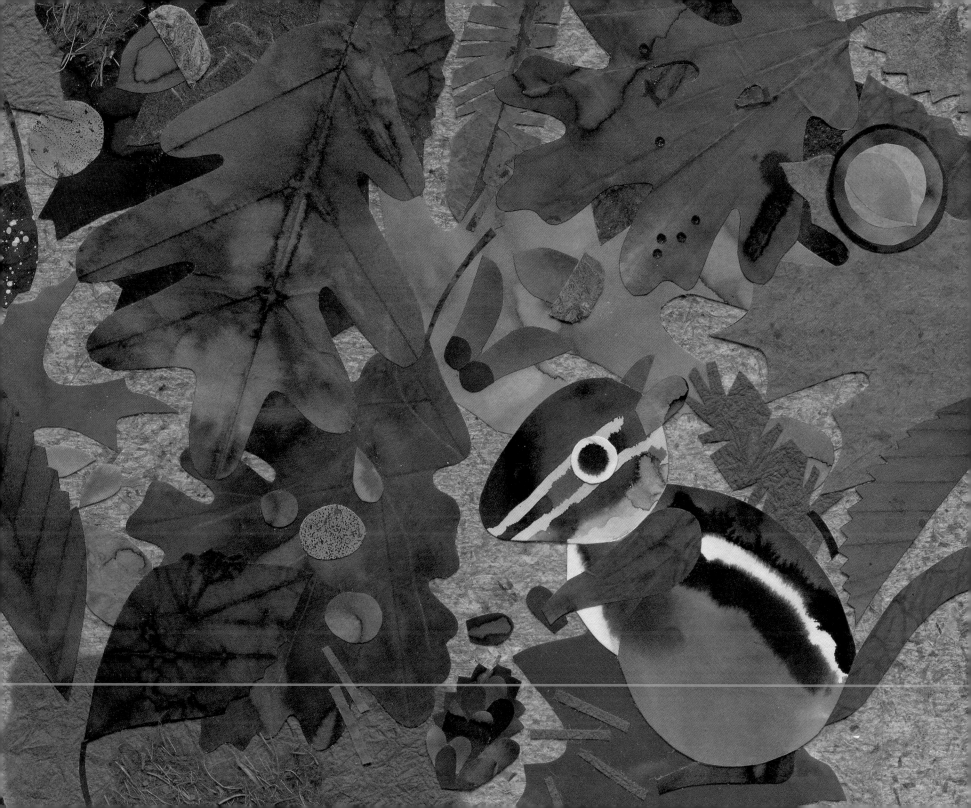

Milkweed
Angels

We lay in the field,

sun blazing on the edge

of milkweed pods.

Wind teased black seeds out,

each a tiny flier

in the sky.

Harvest
Angel

We gathered from the garden—

squash, pumpkins, the last

zucchini—and left them

on the porch. Next morning

a garden angel danced

on the wood.

Leaf Angels

Orange and red and rust

drift down on green grass,

a patchwork stitched

by the quick

steps of blackbirds.

Can you see

ragged coats

spread across the grass?

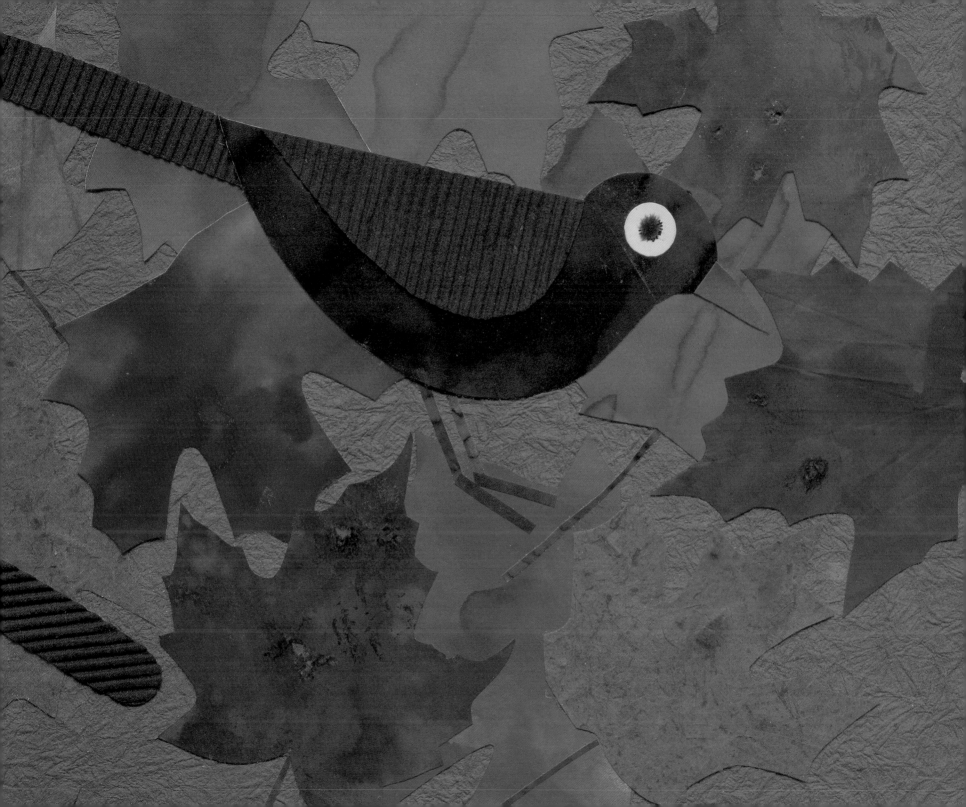

Fire Angels

In the fireplace

red flames burn

bark and wood.

There I see a dress

of orange; here

a halo of yellow.

Suddenly, they fly

up my chimney!

Snow
Angels

You know snow angels;

lie on your back,

swing arms wide

from side to side.

When we leave to go

inside, do they fly

into the air

like a silver song?

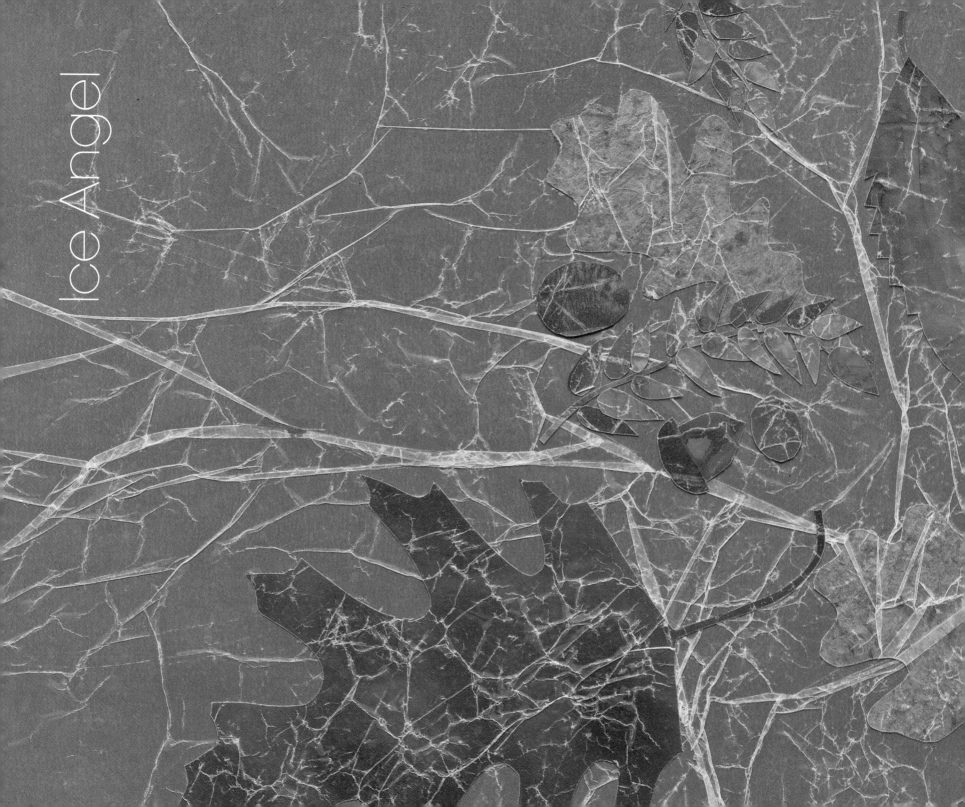

Ice Angel

Under my skates,

I see leaves, twigs, and acorns

frozen in ice.

When spring comes,

where will the angel go?

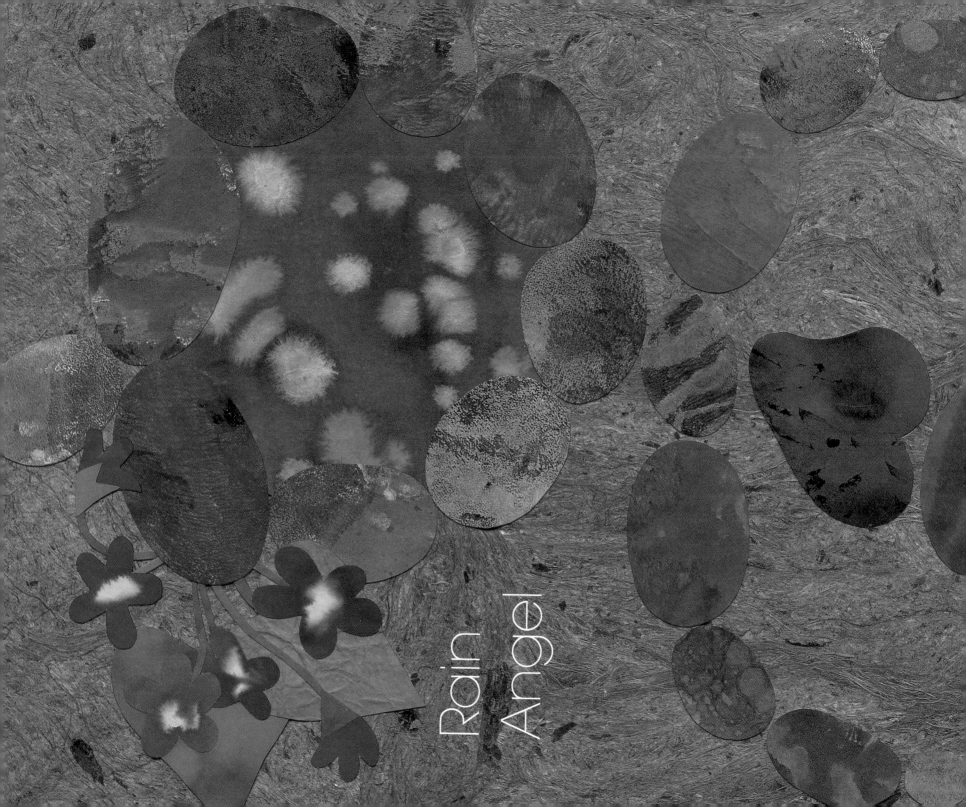

Rain
Angel

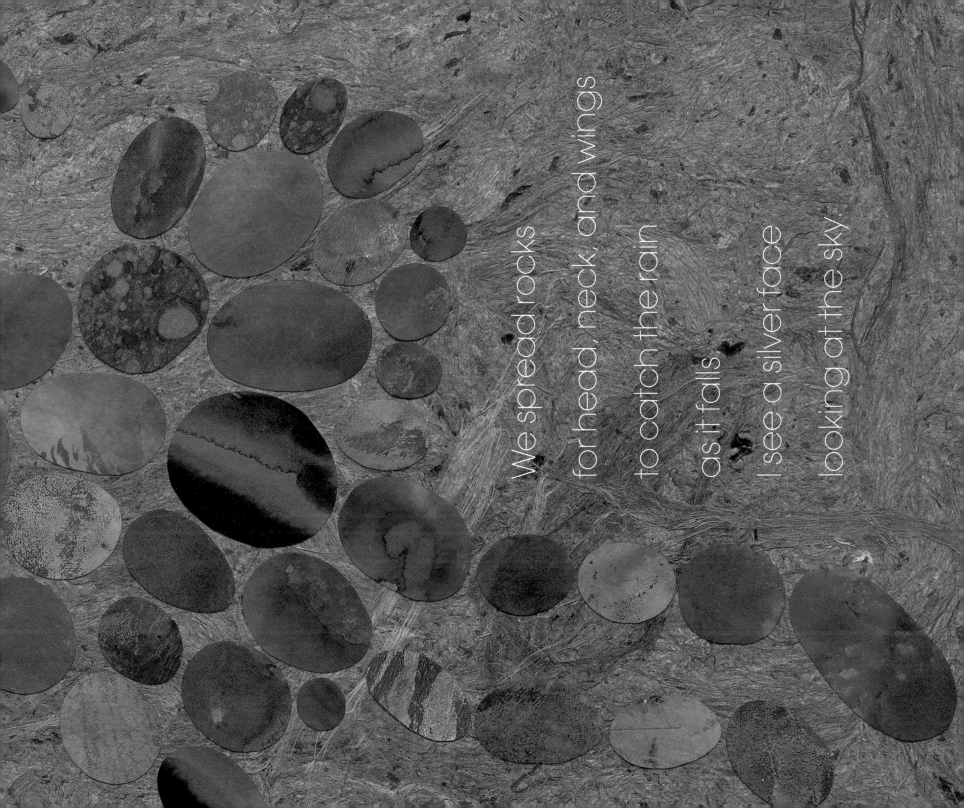

We spread rocks

for head, neck, and wings

to catch the rain

as it falls.

I see a silver face

looking at the sky.

Desert Angel

Where the cactus stands,
a woodpecker bored holes,
a mouse chewed a line,
and sun dried a face
to guard the desert.

Pond
Angel

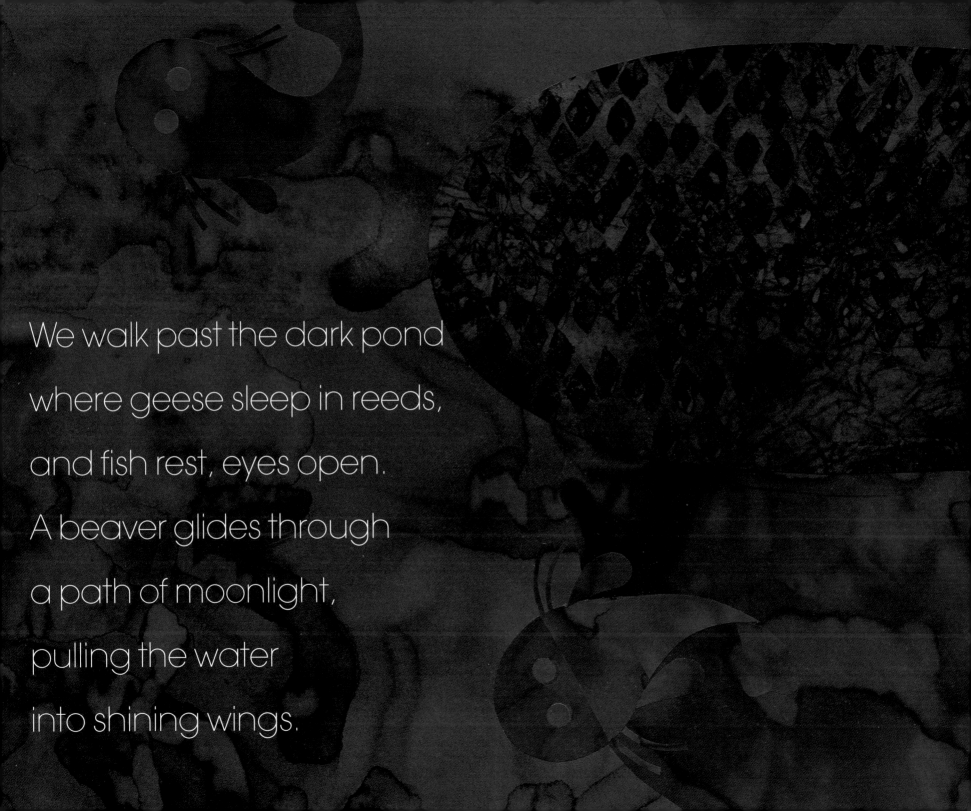

We walk past the dark pond

where geese sleep in reeds,

and fish rest, eyes open.

A beaver glides through

a path of moonlight,

pulling the water

into shining wings.

Cloud Angels

Clouds float over mountains,

white mist streams

like hair and wings.

I think I hear singing

far away.

SUNFLOWER ANGELS

There are many varieties of sunflowers. They're easy to grow from seeds. At the end of the growing season, you can harvest seeds from the flower head. Save them to feed the birds. Sunflowers attract butterflies, like monarchs. Bees suck nectar from the flowers to make honey.

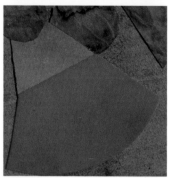

BARN ANGELS

The red flower you see here is a hollyhock. Its flowers grow clustered on tall stalks that sway in warm breezes. Hollyhocks love full sun. Plant them next to a wall or door so they can lean against it. Pick a flower. Turn it upside down. Do you think it looks like a green-headed angel in a pink dress?

HAY ANGEL

Blue chicory, pinkish milkweed blossoms, yellow black-eyed Susans, droopy yellow petals of prairie coneflowers, growing wild, add color to the green and gold of farm fields. Black-eyed Susans and coneflowers are related to sunflowers. Queen Anne's lace is a wild carrot, an ancestor of our garden carrots.

BUTTERFLY ANGEL

The striped monarch caterpillar depends solely on milkweed leaves for food. After eating, it bonds itself to the underside of a leaf and begins making a green sac called a chrysalis (KRIS-uh-lis). Once enclosed, it grows into a monarch butterfly, splits open the chrysalis, pumps its wings, and flies away.

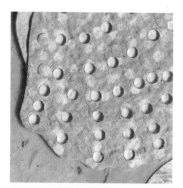

SEA ANGEL

Walking along a sandy shore, you may find treasures washed up by Atlantic Ocean waves. A horseshoe crab, whose shell is used for the angel's head, sheds its shell many times as it grows. Shells used here as wings are named angel wings. The dress and legs are scallop, snail, and clam shells, and her big feet are oyster shells.

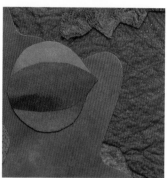

WOOD ANGELS

The woods provide food for animals. Hickory nuts bounce down, cracking the outer shells and exposing the whitish inner shells, which contain a tasty nutmeat. Dry leaves flutter to the ground. Acorns fall from oak trees, cones drop from pine branches, winged seeds from maple trees drift like flying angels.

MILKWEED ANGELS

These wildflowers grow pods that split open in the fall, releasing many seeds, each attached to a soft tuft of white hair. At the slightest breeze, these angels fly away to deposit their seeds. Fields glow with yellow goldenrod and bright-purple wild asters. Did you find the empty chrysalis?

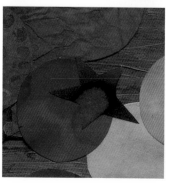

HARVEST ANGEL

As the growing season ends, fruits and vegetables are gathered in from fields and gardens. Green watermelon, broccoli, zucchini; red peppers; a warty red-orange Hubbard squash; an orange pumpkin for Halloween; striped and spotted squash; the last ripe red and yellow tomatoes— a feast for the eyes and stomach.

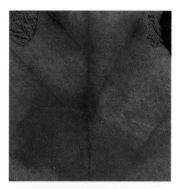

LEAF ANGELS

Cooler air, driving rains, whistling winds tell us winter is coming. Maple trees that a few weeks ago wore golden-red leaf crowns are now almost bare. Pick up a beautiful leaf. Take it home and press it in a book. When winter arrives, you'll have a spot of color to warm you.

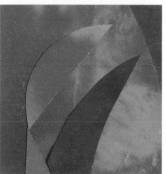

FIRE ANGELS

By the time frost forms lacy ice patterns on windows, many birds have migrated south. Squirrels and rabbits have fur to keep them warm. But you need warm clothes and shelter. After being outside, come in, warm icy hands, stomp numb feet before a blazing fire. Watch for dancing angels.

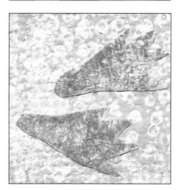

SNOW ANGELS

You can tell which animals live near you by looking for tracks after a new snow. The big tracks shown are squirrel tracks. Squirrels set down their hind feet ahead of their fore-feet when they leap. The cluster of small tracks are bird tracks, maybe cardinals. It's a good time to put out some sunflower seeds for them.

ICE ANGEL

Pools of water, dead leaves, twigs, seeds, and other fall leftovers are frozen solid. It's too late to rake leaves. They are locked into place as if asleep, until spring sun thaws them out. Look for smooth, thick ice with no lumps or cracks. It's time to go ice-skating.

RAIN ANGEL

Spring sun warms the earth, thaws cold ground, and starts the plants and flowers sprouting. If you planted bulbs last fall, you'll soon see green tips breaking through the ground. One important thing they all need, besides the sun, is water. Purple violets open; angel faces drink water from the sky.

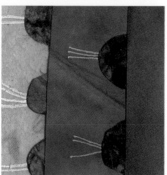

DESERT ANGEL

It doesn't often rain in the Sonoran desert, where the saguaro (suh-WAR-oh), the largest cactus, lives, so it stores up every drop of water under its skin. Gila (HEE-luh) woodpeckers bore holes in the cactus to make their nests. The cactus forms a callus, sealing the inside of the hole so moisture cannot evaporate.

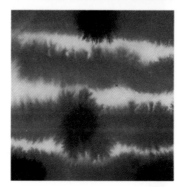

POND ANGEL

Water provides a wet home for many fish, including the whiskered catfish. The beaver lives on the edge of the water. See his flat, scaly tail? He uses it as a rudder as he swims away. Beavers have powerful teeth. They gnaw on trees until they fall, and then use them to build dams.

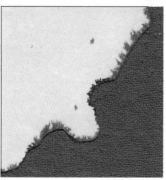

CLOUD ANGELS

The clouds and the color of the sky change with the seasons. Some clouds are filled with rain or snow. The clouds you see here are light, fluffy spring clouds. They move across the blue sky, driven by gusts of warm wind. Stop for a moment. Look up. Do you see angels?

Halo nods,
wing unbends,
I see angels
without end.

Sky, earth,
cloud, and rain,
show your face
to me again.